02/2018

MARC BROWN
ARTHUR'S READING TRICK

Random House 🏠 New York

Visit us on the Web! StepIntoReading.com randomhousekids.com

Educators and librarians, for a variety of teaching tools, visit us at RHTeachersLibrarians.com

Library of Congress Cataloging-in-Publication Data
Brown, Marc Tolon.
Arthur's reading trick / Marc Brown. — 1st ed.
p. cm. — (Step into reading. Step 3 reader)
Summary: Arthur's sister D.W. tries to use a reading trick to get Arthur to change Baby Kate's diapers.
ISBN 978-0-375-82977-2 (trade pbk.) — ISBN 978-0-375-92977-9 (lib. bdg.)
[1. Reading—Fiction. 2. Brothers and sisters—Fiction. 3. Babies—Fiction. 4. Aardvark—Fiction.] I. Title.
PZ7.B81618Arqb 2009
[E]—dc22 2008050979

Printed in the United States of America 19 18 17 16 15 14 13 12 11

This book has been officially leveled by using the F&P Text Level Gradient™ Leveling System.

D.W. could say her ABCs.

She could write them too.

And she could read one book,

Green Eggs and *Ham*.

She liked to read it to Arthur.

"Oh, no," said Arthur.

"Not again!"

"I bet I can teach Baby Kate
to read," said D.W.
"I bet you can't," said Arthur.
"And the loser has to change
Kate's stinky diaper."
"It's a deal," said D.W.

"Work on it," said Arthur,

"while I do my homework."

D.W. got her crayons
and some paper.

She got Kate's red ball
with stars.

She got Kate's little blue car.

And she got Kate's bottle.

D.W. wrote the letters B-A-L-L
on the paper.

Then she held up the red ball
and pointed to the letters.

"What does this say, Kate?"
asked D.W.

"Ball!" said Kate.

Next D.W. wrote C-A-R.

She held up the blue car.

"What do these letters say?"

D.W. asked Kate.

"Car!" said Kate.

D.W. did the same thing
with Kate's bottle.
And Kate said, "Bottle!"
"Mom, come here," shouted D.W.
"Kate can read!"

"Watch this, Mom," said D.W.
She held up
the ball and the paper
with the letters B-A-L-L.
Kate said, "Ball!"

D.W. did the same thing
with the car and the bottle.
Kate said, "Car!" and "Bottle!"
"See, Mom," said D.W.
"I taught Kate how to read."

Mom smiled and shook her head.

"No, D.W.," said Mom.

"Kate is just saying words
she knows
when she sees those objects.
In two years
you can try teaching her."

Mom went back to her computer.

D.W. thought about changing
stinky diapers.

Then she had an idea.

D.W. put the ball and the car
in her pockets.
She hid the bottle
under the sofa.
"Arthur," she called
up the stairs.
"I taught Kate to read."

"This I have to see,"
said Arthur.
"Hold this paper
in front of Kate,"
D.W. told Arthur.
"Now point to the letters."
D.W. stood behind Arthur.
She held up the ball.
"Ball!" said Kate.

BALL

Then D.W. gave him
the paper with the letters C-A-R.
Arthur held it up.
D.W. stood behind Arthur
and waved the car at Kate.
"Car!" said Kate.
"I won the bet," said D.W.
"It's stinky diapers for you!"

"Not so fast, D.W.," said Arthur.

"Let's try another word."

"Okay, I don't mind," said D.W.

She handed him the paper

with the letters B-O-T-T-L-E.

But Kate's bottle had rolled

way under the sofa.

"Wait a minute," said D.W.

"I'm not ready."

Then Arthur knew D.W.'s trick.

But he had a trick of his own.

He picked up a diaper

from a box of clean diapers.

He held up the paper

with the letters B-O-T-T-L-E.

"What do the letters say, Kate?"

He waved the diaper.

"Diaper!" said Kate.

BOTTLE

BALL

DIAPERS

.ELIZA.

23

"I win," said Arthur.

"And it smells like

Kate needs a clean one, D.W."

"Oh, no!" cried D.W.